Those Kooky Kangaroos

Bonnie Nickel

Illustrations by Steve Weaver

Pineapple Press, Inc.

Sarasota, Florida

Photo Credits
Cover photo: ©Kitch/Dreamstime.com; Page 2: ©Bgphoto/Dreamstime.com; Page 5: ©Susanne Ulyatt; Page 8: ©Stokaji/Dreamstime.com; Page 10: red kangaroo ©Musat/Dreamstime.com, grey kangaroo ©Krystof/Dreamstime.com, yellow-footed rock wallaby ©Benmm/Dreamstime.com, Matschie's tree kangaroo ©Photoleaf/Dreamstime.com, quokka ©Jlye/Dreamstime.com, black-striped wallaby ©Susanne Ulyatt, red-necked pademelon ©Susanne Ulyatt; Page 12: ©Joeygil/Dreamstime.com; Page 14: ©Benmm/Dreamstime.com; Page 16: red kangaroo ©Twildlife/Dreamstime.com, quokka ©Kitch/Dreamstime.com; Page 18: ©Redzaal/Dreamstime.com; Page 22: ©Perception/Dreamstime.com; Page 24: ©Mato750/Dreamstime.com; Page 26: grey kangaroo ©Ajcmeehan/Dreamstime.com, tree kangaroo ©Iorboaz/Dreamstime.com; Page 28: ©Sandbread/Dreamstime.com; Page 30: ©Rhyspope/Dreamstime.com; Page 32: ©Silvavj/Dreamstime.com; Page 34: ©Zerojeden/Dreamstime.com; Page 36: ©Kitch/Dreamstime.com; Page 38: ©Nazdav/Dreamstime.com; Page 40: ©Flynt/Dreamstime.com; Page 42: grey kangaroo ©Kitch/Dreamstime.com, red-necked wallaby ©Susanne Ulyatt, red-necked pademelon ©Susanne Ulyatt; Page 44: ©Jacquimartin/Dreamstime.com; Page 46: ©Robynmac/Dreamstime.com; Page 52: ©Susanne Ulyatt.

Inquiries should be addressed to:

Pineapple Press, Inc.
P.O. Box 3889
Sarasota, Florida 34230
www.pineapplepress.com

Library of Congress Cataloging-in-Publication Data
Nickel, Bonnie
  Those kooky kangaroos / Bonnie Nickel. -- 1st ed.
     p. cm.
  Includes index.
  ISBN 978-1-56164-534-3 (hardcover : alk. paper) -- ISBN 978-1-56164-535-0 (pbk. : alk. paper)
1. Kangaroos--Juvenile literature. I. Title.
  QL737.M35N53 2012
  599.2'22--dc23
                                    2012016034

First Edition
Hb 10 9 8 7 6 5 4 3 2 1
Pb 10 9 8 7 6 5 4 3 2 1

Printed in Singapore

To Kim

Special thanks to Bryan, Nicole, and Ula Cierniak for their assistance with this book.

Contents

What is a kangaroo?

Kangaroos are a kooky type of mammal. Look at those small front legs. And those very large back legs, tails, and ears. They are warm-blooded and furry, but they don't look, walk, or run like other mammals. Their babies are peculiar too. Newborns are tiny. They grow up in a pouch on their mother's belly. Mammals that grow like this are marsupials. Kangaroos belong to a group of marsupials called macropods. Macro means big. Pod means foot. They're well-named!

1) red kangaroo

2) grey kangaroo

3) yellow-footed rock wallaby

4) Matschie's tree kangaroo

5) quokka

6) black-striped wallaby

7) red-necked pademelon

How many kinds of macropods are there?

Lots! There are about 60 species. There are large macropods—red kangaroos, Eastern grey kangaroos, and Western grey kangaroos. There are small macropods including pademelons, wallabies, and quokkas. There are 'tweeners—wallaroos—the name is a combination of wallaby and kangaroo. And there are 10 species of tree kangaroos. All are commonly called "kangaroos" as they are in this book. Their fur can be solid, or patterned with brown, black, blue, gray, red, yellow, white, orange, even purple markings!

11

What's a nabarlek?

A type of wallaby. Over 30 of the 60 macropod species are wallabies. Other wallaby names include rock, hare, swamp, parma, nailtail, tammar, and black forest wallabies. That's a lot of wallabies! The monjon, rufous hare, and nabarlek wallabies are the smallest—only 2–3 pounds. Some wallabies live in rocky areas—they are agile and have rough-soled feet for gripping the rocks.

Do kangaroos have cousins?

Yes. There are over 240 other species of marsupials—mammals that give birth to tiny babies that grow in a pouch on their mother's belly. Other marsupials include wombats, numbats, possums, potoroos, bettongs, bandicoots, bilbies, and the Tasmanian Devil. One of the best known marsupials is the koala. It is often called a koala bear, but it's not related to bears. The only marsupial that lives in North America is the Virginia opossum.

red kangaroo

quokka

How big are kangaroos?

Big—the largest is the red kangaroo. The adult male can be 120–200 pounds and 9 feet long including its tail. Their feet are up to 18 inches long! And small—wallabies can be 2 to 50 pounds. Many are the size of a large house cat. Wallaroos are bigger than wallabies but smaller than kangaroos. That's how they got their name! Females are usually smaller than males, sometimes half the size. Most kangaroos continue to grow their whole lives.

What is a kangaroo mob?

A group of kangaroos. The average mob size is about 10, but hundreds can gather where there's lots of food. Larger kangaroos are more likely to live together, but whiptail wallabies are the most social. They live in groups of 30 to 50. Hare, swamp, and nailtail wallabies like to live alone. Mothers and babies are more likely to be found in groups. They are safer together—some watch for danger while others eat or rest.

Papua New Guinea

Australia

Tasmania

Where in the world do kangaroos live?

Kangaroo

 Wallaby and/or Wallaroo

 Tree Kangaroo

Ranges for individual species vary. Some ranges are quite large (wallaroos); some are quite small (most wallabies and tree kangaroos).

Most wild kangaroos live on the continent of Australia. Some live on islands like Tasmania, New Guinea, and smaller islands around Australia. Kangaroos can be found in deserts, forests, mountains, rainforests, and grasslands. Large kangaroos live in grasslands with trees for shade. Reds live in hot desert areas. Wallabies live in forested areas. Rock wallabies live in rocky hillsides. Bennett's wallabies dig tunnels in the snow of Tasmania. Brrr!

Goodfellow's tree kangaroo

Do kangaroos live in trees?

Only tree kangaroos! They look like small bears and act like monkeys. Their front legs and tails are longer, and their ears are small and furry. They climb on all fours through the trees. They can even walk backwards unlike other kangaroos. Tree kangaroos can survive crash landings from as far as 60 feet up! They live in the mountain forests of New Guinea, Australia, and a few small islands. Some live in mountains as high as 14,000 feet.

What are boomers, fliers, and stinkers?

Kangaroo nicknames! Baby kangaroos are called joeys. Male kangaroos are boomers or bucks. Female red kangaroos are blue fliers. They are bluish-gray and very fast. Females are also called does, just like deer. Male western grey kangaroos are called stinkers because they smell like curry. Whew! If a mob has a dominant male, he is the old man. Nailtail wallabies are called organ grinders. Their front legs move in circles when they run.

grey kangaroo

tree kangaroo

How do kangaroos get around?

Kangaroos are one of the few mammals that travel on 2 legs. They use their powerful back legs to hop. They can easily hop 12–15 miles per hour. Large kangaroos can hop 35-40 miles per hour when they're in a hurry. When moving slowly, they don't walk like other animals. They balance on their front legs and tail, then swing their back feet forward. Their back feet always move together except when swimming. Tree kangaroos walk on four legs.

Are kangaroos spring-loaded?

In a way. Large kangaroos can jump as far as 30 feet in a single hop. They can jump as high as 10 feet. Their back legs have tendons that act like a spring or an elastic band. The faster they hop, the farther the springs send them. And it's easy for them! Hopping helps to push air in and out of their lungs so they don't run out of breath. Kangaroos can even change direction in mid-hop using their tail to steer.

What do kangaroos eat?

Kangaroos are herbivores—they eat plants. Large kangaroos are grazers. They eat mostly grass. Pademelons, tree kangaroos, and swamp wallabies are browsers. They eat grass, leaves, bark, and fruit. Kangaroos have stomach bacteria to break down the tough plants. They have special front teeth for biting off the plants and big back molars to grind their food. Grinding is hard on their teeth. The front molars wear down and fall out. A new set grows in from the back.

Do kangaroos drink water?

Not much. They get most of the water they need from the plants they eat. Red kangaroos and rock wallabies can go months without drinking. When the tammar wallaby can't find fresh water, it drinks salt water from the sea. Eewh! The spectacled hare wallaby doesn't drink water at all. It only gets water from the food it eats.

Why do kangaroos box?

They usually have a pretty good reason. Large male kangaroos may fight each other for favorite foods, shady sleeping spots, or female kangaroos. They punch or hold each other with their short front legs. Then they balance on their tail and kick with their strong back legs. Ouch! They don't box often and the fight is usually over quickly. The weaker (but smart!) kangaroo may cluck or cough to show he doesn't want to fight.

Are kangaroos good listeners?

Yes. Kangaroos need to stay alert for danger—dingoes, hawks, snakes, and humans. They can rotate their large ears around so they can hear from any side. Kangaroos that live in mobs take turns listening for danger while the others eat and tend their young. A mother will cluck to call her joey back to the pouch. Smaller wallabies and pademelons thump their back feet like a rabbit, warning others of danger. Hare wallabies whistle when they are in danger.

Are kangaroos lazy?

You might think so if you saw them only during the day. Kangaroos spend the day resting and sleeping in the shade. They sleep for short periods taking turns being the lookout. They are nocturnal. They spend the night eating and traveling around. They are most active at dawn and dusk. Most don't wander far from their home areas unless food runs low. Red kangaroos and young male kangaroos are most likely to move from their home range.

Are kangaroos cool?

They try to be! Most kangaroos live in hot climates. They lie in the shade during the hottest time of the day. They eat at night when it is cool. Rock wallabies spend the day hiding in cool caves and crevices. Kangaroos sweat when they hop. When they stop, they pant through their noses, unlike dogs that pant through their mouths. Kangaroos lick their front legs. The breeze evaporates the water and carries the heat away. It works like built-in air conditioning!

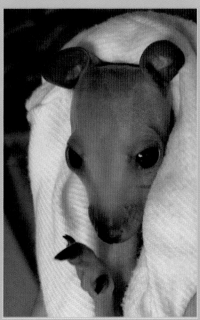

What do baby kangaroos look like?

Like all marsupials, newborn kangaroos are tiny—the size of a jelly bean or smaller. They are blind, deaf, and pink, with no hair or tail. Only their front legs are developed—they use them to climb into their mother's pouch. It's a long trip for a tiny joey! They nurse in the pouch and grow bigger, until they look like small kangaroos. Kangaroos have one joey at a time. When one leaves the pouch, the next one moves in.

How long do joeys stay in the pouch?

Joeys grow in the pouch for 3 to 4 months before they poke their heads out. They look around and watch other kangaroos. By about 5 to 6 months they crawl out. They stay close to mom. She calls her joey back often so it learns to sense danger. Joeys will dive back into the pouch head first and turn right-side up. After 10 to 18 months joeys have grown enough to stop nursing and live outside the pouch.

dingo

What are the dangers to kangaroos?

Small wallabies and tree kangaroos are endangered because their forests are cut down and they are hunted for food. Joeys and small wallabies are hunted by dingoes, eagles, foxes, dogs, and cats. Wallabies compete for food with introduced animals like sheep, rabbits, and goats. Reds, greys, and wallaroos are not endangered, but they are hunted for fur, meat, and as pests. Many are also hit by cars. As the planet warms, drought and wildfires increase and kangaroo habitat dries out.

Activities
Make a Kangaroo

What you will need:
- toilet paper roll or half a paper towel roll
- cereal box or other light cardboard
- glue, stapler, scissors
- pens, pencils, or markers
- fabric or felt (optional)

1. Staple the top of the paper roll closed. Round off the outside edges. This is the body of your kangaroo.
2. Cut 2 cardboard strips, 3 inches by ½ inch, for back feet.
3. Cut a small notch on either side of one end so your kangaroo has 2 long middle toes. Draw in the toes with pen or marker.
4. Glue the feet to the bottom of your paper roll.
5. Cut 2 cardboard strips, 1 ¼ inches by ¼ inch, for front feet.
6. Draw toes on the front legs.
7. Cut 2 small slits about one inch down from the top of your kangaroo.
8. Insert the front legs.
9. Cut one small and one large oval with ears for the heads.
10. Draw in the faces. Draw a line on the paper roll for the pouch.
11. Glue the large head on the top and the small head above the pouch.
12. Cut a 3 inch curved tail from cardboard.
13. Cut a small slit in the back of the paper roll and insert the tail.

Kangaroos come in many shades so color your kangaroo with pencils, crayons, or even fabric. Use your imagination!

Hop Like a Kangaroo

How do you compare to the red kangaroo? Its feet are up to 18 inches long and it can jump up to 30 feet in a single hop. Let's see how you measure up.

What you will need:
- chalk
- place markers, for example little flags
- tape measure or ruler

Measuring Kangaroo Hops
1. Measure 30 feet with your ruler or tape measure.
2. Mark the start and finish with a flag or marker.
3. Line up both feet side by side at the first line.
4. Jump with your feet together, your arms bent like a kangaroo.
5. Jump all the way to the second marker and count each hop.
6. How many hops do you need for one kangaroo hop?

Measuring Kangaroo Feet
1. Use chalk to draw a kangaroo foot 18 inches long.
2. Make the 2 middle toes longer than the 2 outer toes.
3. Walk your feet one in front of the other and count your steps.
4. How many of your feet fit in the footprint of a big red kangaroo?

Find a Wallaby

There are over 30 species of wallabies. Wallabies are the smallest of the macropods. See if you can find these wallaby names in the puzzle. Circle each one in the puzzle as you find it and check it off the list.

Agile   Parma
Hare   Rednecked
Monjon   Swamp
Nailtail   Tammar
Pademelon   Whiptail

```
                        N N
                      O D A U                      P R
                  J G E I H T              H A R E
N             N F H K L S A H E M R B
   B             D O E J I C T I B N M W M
      C N O L E M E D A P E A C G A S G A
               K L S O N I P T A M O R
               N M R D L J T S V
               D L E S        F
               R W          I
               K A
               P M
               L P
               W H I P T A I L
```

Hint: Words can appear in any direction—forward, backward, up, down, even on an angle. Try searching for the first letter of a word, then look all around it for the second letter and follow in that direction to see if you're right. If not, look for the first letter again.

Where to Learn More about Kangaroos

Good Books to Read

Endangered Kangaroos by John Woodward, Benchmark Books, New York, 1997.

Kangaroos by Peter Murray, The Child's World, Minnesota, 2006.

Quest for the Tree Kangaroo; An Expedition to the Cloud Forest of New Guinea by Sy Montgomery, Houghton Mifflin Co., Massachusetts, 2006.

Walker's Marsupials of the World by Ronald M. Nowak, The Johns Hopkins University Press, Maryland, 2005.

Good Websites to Visit

The Kangaroo Trail: rootourism.com

Tenkile Conservation Alliance (dedicated to saving tree kangaroos): tenkile.com

University of Michigan Museum of Zoology:

Myers, P. 2001. *Macropodidae* (On-line), Animal Diversity Web. Accessed Nov. 30, 2011 http://animaldiversity. ummz.umich.edu/site/accounts/information/ Macropodidae.html

Wildlife Rescue

Many people volunteer their time rescuing injured or orphaned wildlife. WIRES (Wildlife Information, Rescue and Education Service Inc.) is the largest wildlife rescue and care organization in Australia with over 2000 volunteers. They rescue, rehabilitate, and release birds, reptiles, flying foxes, gliders, possums, platypuses, koalas, bats, and, of course, kangaroos, wallabies, and other marsupials. A special thanks to Susanne Ulyatt at the Northern Rivers branch for her help with this book. Visit their website at wiresnr.org to learn more about what they do. Find out where your closest wildlife rescue group is and ask them how you can help.

Glossary

agile – able to move quickly and easily

bacteria – very tiny single cells that live almost everywhere

climate – average weather of a place

continent – a large land mass on the planet

crevice – a narrow opening or crack

curry – a strong-smelling (but yummy) spice used in cooking

dominant – controls what others do

evaporate – when water moves from a surface to the air

habitat – the area where an animal lives

introduced – brought in to a new place

mammal – warm-blooded, furry animals

marsupial – a mammal that has underdeveloped young that develop in a pouch outside the body

organ grinder – someone who cranks a musical hand organ

patterned – made up of stripes, dots, or other marks

rotate – to turn around

social – to like being around others

species – a single type of animal or plant within a larger group

tendon – a body part that connects muscles to other muscles or bones

Jim Nickel

About the Author

Bonnie is the author of *Those Mischievous Monkeys*, also in the series *Those Amazing Animals*. She teaches people about conservation and sustainability—how to use less water, electricity, fuel, and other stuff—so that humans, animals (including kangaroos!), trees, and plants can all share the planet and pass it along to the next generation. Originally from Canada, Bonnie now lives in Florida with her husband Jim and their two kooky dogs, Cooper and Joie.

Index

Photographs are indicated by boldface type.

Here are the other books in this series. Each title in the Those Amazing Animals series, written for children ages 6–9, has 20 questions and answers, 20 photos, and 20 funny illustrations by Steve Weaver. For a complete catalog, visit our website at www.pineapplepress.com.

Those Amazing Alligators by Kathy Feeney. Discover the differences between alligators and crocodiles. Learn what alligators eat, how they communicate, and much more.

Those Beautiful Butterflies by Sarah Cussen. Learn all about butterflies—their behavior, why they look the way they do, how they communicate, and why they love bright flowers.

Those Big Bears by Jan Lee Wicker. Why do bears stand on two legs? How do they use their claws? How many kinds are there? What do they do all winter?

Those Colossal Cats by Marta Magellan. Meet lions, tigers, leopards, and the other big cats. Do they purr? How fast can they run? Which is biggest?

Those Delightful Dolphins by Jan Lee Wicker. Dolphins are delightful in the way they communicate and play with one another and the way they cooperate with humans.

Those Enormous Elephants by Sarah Cussen. Find out how elephants' ears act as air conditioners. Learn the difference between African and Asian elephants. Discover how elephants care for sick and old members of the group.

Those Excellent Eagles by Jan Lee Wicker. Learn all about those excellent eagles—what they eat, how fast they fly, why the American bald eagle is our nation's national bird.

Those Funny Flamingos by Jan Lee Wicker. Why are these funny birds pink? Why do they stand on one leg and eat upside down? Where do they live?

Those Lively Lizards by Marta Magellan. Meet lizards that can run on water, some with funny-looking eyes, some that change color, and some that look like little dinosaurs.

Those Magical Manatees by Jan Lee Wicker. Why are they magical? How big are they? What do they eat? Why are they endangered and what can you do to help?

Those Mischievous Monkeys by Bonnie Nickel. Find out where in the world monkeys live, what they eat, and what they do for fun.

Those Outrageous Owls by Laura Wyatt. Learn what owls eat, how they hunt, and why they look the way they do. How do they fly so quietly? Why do horned owls have horns?

Those Peculiar Pelicans by Sarah Cussen. Find out how much food those peculiar pelicans can fit in their beaks, how they stay cool, and whether they really steal fish from fishermen.

Those Perky Penguins by Sarah Cussen. Can penguins fly? Do they get cold? How many kinds are there and where in the world do they live?

Those Terrific Turtles by Sarah Cussen. You'll learn the difference between a turtle and a tortoise and find out why they have shells. Meet baby turtles and some very, very old ones.

Those Voracious Vultures by Marta Magellan. Learn all about vultures—the gross things they do, what they eat, whether a turkey vulture gobbles, and more.